Echoes from the Dark Forest

Author: Briana Blye

Publisher: Amazon KDP

Date of Publication: 2024

Copyright © 2024

Copyright © 2024 by Briana Blye

All rights reserved. No part of this book may be reproduced, stored in a retrieval system, or transmitted in any form or by any means—electronic, mechanical, photocopying, recording, or otherwise—without prior written permission of the publisher, except for brief quotations embodied in critical articles and reviews.

Published by Amazon.com

Printed in USA

ISBN: 9798335645409

First Edition: 2024

Cover design by Briana Blye

Editing by Briana Blye

Disclaimer: The characters, incidents, and dialogue in this book are products of the author's imagination or are used fictitiously. Any resemblance to actual events or persons, living or dead, is entirely coincidental.

Visit Amazon.com for more information about the author and upcoming releases.

This book is dedicated to my family and friends, whose support has been the foundation of my journey as a writer. Thank you for believing in me, even when I doubted myself.

To my readers, your love for stories inspires my creativity. Thank you for opening these pages and stepping into the world I've created.

And finally, to anyone who has ever dreamed of something bigger than themselves—keep dreaming, keep smiling, keep writing, and never stop believing.

With my deepest gratitude,

Briana Blye

Table of Contents

Sunset 4
The Oak Tree 7
Ascend 11
Candlelight 15
Dawn 21
Morning Dew 25
A Ritual Guide 31
Dougal 33
Cole 37
The Secret Path 46
Hours 47
Jennifer 54
The Girl in the Purple Dress 61
Tears 66
Confession 72
The Plan 79
Creatures of the Night 86
Witches 89
Never Cross a Witch 101

Sunset

My friends and I stumbled through the darkening forest as the sun was setting slowly behind us. Our shadows looked like creatures of a nightmare coming to life, running alongside our bodies. The leaves of the trees swayed slightly in the breeze, cooling the sweat from our foreheads. It felt like we had been running for miles when we stumbled upon the old, eerie castle in the woods. This was the first time I had seen something like it. As children, we heard stories about what may dwell within, but no one ever really believed those tales. There were stories of witches that would cast spells on the young children who snuck inside uninvited, and sometimes they were never seen or heard from again. Someone at school a few years back said there was an evil cult of human-animal creatures that hunted at night to feast upon the humans living in surrounding towns. Although the stories were creepy and definitely great for scaring people, I never let them bother me.

As we stopped among the roots of a giant oak tree, my friends laughed about investigating what may lie hidden just beyond the rusty gate. I studied the building from afar, unsure of how close I wanted to get. The gate looked as though it had been painted a soft, white color some time ago, but it had been rusting with an ugly, green moss. The castle itself was larger than life, with columns holding up a balcony from either side of the giant doors. The peaks along the top reminded me of something medieval, each having its window for one to admire the landscape from high above. The creamy, white paint that matched the fence was peeling back in layers from different areas on the face of the old structure. Former light fixtures still hung from where they had been placed during the construction of the castle.

"Let's go!" Cassie yelled from the left side of the oak tree.

"She's too scared!" Jennifer said, pointing a finger in my direction.

I shook my head, "I'm not scared, but you two don't believe the tales we were told when we were young."

Cassie laughed, "No such evil lives inside that place. It's been abandoned for years."

Jennifer didn't make a sound, she just nodded in agreement with Cassie's statement, her eyebrows raised high above her eyes.

I shrugged as I glanced back toward the castle, "Maybe another time."

Cassie wiped sweat from her forehead, "Whatever, it's getting pretty dark, so we should probably head back."

Cassie and Jennifer turned around, headed for the oak tree and began walking gleefully back toward town. I waited until they were out of sight before hiding myself behind the tree, directly in line with the castle. It was magnificent, unlike anything I had ever seen. I felt an immediate connection with it like a moth to a flame. It was almost like the castle was calling out to me, summoning me to come closer.

The Oak Tree

  The full moon rose in the sky, glowing brighter than it ever had, revealing the sleeping earth below. I lay in my bed thinking about the castle. A fresh breeze blew in through my window, sweeping across my cheek. I wondered if evil lived within, or if those tales were told only to scare us as children. I never ventured out much when I was a child. I was always ordered to take my older brother Ryan along with me if I were to go anywhere. My parents made it seem as if the world were unsafe to explore alone. Whenever my imagination got the best of me, I'd find myself talking about the things that thrived in the forest or just along the riverbed. I'd count the stars from my window and draw pictures of the fireflies glowing in the summer heat. I snuck out when I was 16, but it was only to meet up with Jennifer and a boy that I liked.

  Now at 21, I enjoy sitting by the river, feeling the cool water flowing over my feet and between my toes. I lived for moments when I could read books in the trees, high above the rest of the forest while listening to the birds as they sing. I guess what it comes down to is that nature has given me the things that people cannot. It gives me the things I don't believe people can provide - happiness, peace, tranquility, and freedom. It may be possible to feel those things when around someone, but I do not believe we have the power to fully provide them for another human being. It is physically, mentally, and emotionally impossible. Nature, on the other hand, provides all of those things and more, forever. It's the red and orange sunsets, the purple skies, the heavy rainfall, the electricity of the lightning during a storm, the colorful flowers in the spring, and the green of the summer. One couldn't forget the crisp autumn breeze carrying the decaying leaves from the trees, the whitest of winters spreading snow over the land, and the power of the currents moving water from place to place. Humans don't provide much of anything. Not for me at least. I seek adventure. I have this overwhelming feeling that there's something more awaiting me. Maybe I should venture out to the castle, but I don't need anyone else.

I'll go alone.

...

I made my way out to the oak tree where I had been with Cassie and Jennifer just hours ago. Luckily, the moon was bright enough to lead the way, shining directly down on the long, dark branches of the oak tree. It was one of the largest trees around, so it was always pretty easy to spot. The castle was fairly visible from this point, but I climbed the oak to see it more. The leaves also helped hide me from any night creatures or human travelers. I made myself comfortable, my back leaning on one of the larger branches, and I studied the castle a bit more. It was astonishingly beautiful. The moonlight lit the face of the castle well enough to make out the chipping paint but the light fixtures in front remained dark. Some of the windows closest to the ground were either smashed or cracked enough to let the cool night breeze inside. The moonlight made the castle look blue, and as vast as the ocean. It almost magnified it to a monstrous extent. If I were a night traveler, I may find this place to be uninviting, yet human curiosity is inevitable.

Lost in thought, the bushes rustled to my left distracting me for a moment. I squinted, rubbing my eyes in hopes of a clearer view when something caught my eye. At one of the peaks in the castle, something was illuminated through one of the glass windows high above. The silhouette of what appeared to be a person, or many people, burned with an intense orange, fiery glow from the candlelight. I knew it couldn't be the moon since it wasn't the cool, blue color it had been that night. My curiosity was sparked. If the castle had been abandoned for years, why would there be a source of light? *Who* was this source of light? Was it meant as a signal for help? Could it be a welcoming signal? Is the castle calling out to me?

"Oh, I hope no one has seen me out here in the oak tree," I whispered to myself, nervously clutching a piece of broken bark in my hand.

I wanted to move closer to get a better look at whatever it was I was seeing through that window. Carefully, I climbed down the tree, using the branches as a crutch. Once my feet hit the ground, I quickly and quietly scurried off into the night, headed for the castle.

Ascend

Other than the rusty, old gate outlining the overgrown grass in the yard, there was also a huge stone wall that covered the areas around the sides and the back of the castle. I paced around the side of the stone wall, trying to find an easy entry point. There have been people over the years exploring and destroying the place, so the wires along the top of the stone have been cut completely, allowing people to get over safely. I'm sure the wire played an important role in keeping people out in the past, but now it is next to impossible to do so. The light from the moon showed on the wall and I used my hands to feel for any cracks I may be able to get my foot inside. I ascended the wall carefully, step by step, praying I didn't fall. If I hurt myself out here, who knows when I would be found, if ever? I made my way atop the wall and bent down to rub the debris off the knees of my jeans. I couldn't see the light from this side, so I knew I had to make my way toward the windows. I walked quietly along the wall, keeping watch of my footing while scanning the castle for any sign of movement.

"Where did you go?" I questioned quietly, as if the light would answer me.

I sat down and scooted across the stone until my feet touched the ground. The dry grass cracked beneath my shoes as I reached the castle walls. I paused for a moment and put my hands against the cool, mossy, paint-peeled wall of the castle. A deep sadness washed over me for a place that was once so beautiful. It was heartbreaking to see it in such a decayed state. It deserved more than to be left in the woods, lonely and dead.

I looked around, trying to decide if going inside was my best option. The plan seemed dangerous, but I was up for the adventure. I'd be sure to keep quiet, no matter what might make me scream.

The castle caught me by surprise once I entered through the broken glass window on the lower floor. I found a candlestick lying just below my feet. I pulled my lighter from deep within my pocket and lit it. Luckily, it gave me just enough light to see in front of me. It was eerie to be in an unknown place, alone, with only the candlelight helping to provide any type of sight. The tired, wooden floor groaned beneath my feet as I walked. The humidity that lingered caused my feet to stick to the floor every so often. The walls were painted many different colors in each room I entered and some furniture still remained, ripped and rotted. I covered my nose with my arm to block out the smell of mold that was more than likely growing among the ceilings above. My thoughts came to an immediate pause when I heard an odd sound coming from the floor above where I stood. It sounded as if someone were dragging something heavy against the floorboards. I held my breath and began creeping toward the staircase to ascend onward toward the sound. The stairs were covered with a beautiful, but discolored red carpet. I followed the steps to the very top floor, but I wanted to investigate each room first to be sure I was alone. The pressure of something crawling up the back of my neck began to settle in on me and my mouth grew dry. I reached forward and pushed open the large, brown door in front of me, exposing an empty room. The only piece of furniture was a rocking chair that sat at the window. I checked my surroundings before leaving the room to explore further.

"Where are you?" I whispered into the darkness.

I met the stairs again and again until I ascended them entirely to the very top. Down the long stretch of the hall, I saw the light. It was still glowing, just more faintly than before. I quietly made my way toward it, wondering if I was truly alone. As I approached the room, I noticed it was blocked by a door that looked different than all the others. This door was solid black in color, and there were holes in it that looked like bullets had made their way through at one point in time. There was a strange drawing scratched into the door that appeared to have a long face, hollow eyes, and a wide mouth. I peeked through one of the holes and into the dull-lit room. I couldn't see anything well enough, other than the candlestick that sat in the window.

"Oh, that's what has been glowing this whole time," I said aloud, forgetting the secret mission I had set myself on.

There was a noise from within the room as if someone had just heard me. It was that same odd, scraping sound I had heard earlier. It sounded again like something was being dragged across the floor. Then, there were whispers. They sounded human, but they were so quiet that it was hard to hear what the voices were saying. Trying to calm my nerves I took a deep breath in, reminding myself that this castle had been dead and vacant for years. I reached my hand forward, my curiosity getting the best of me and I knocked.

Candlelight

Knock. Knock. The knocking didn't seem to be working. *Knock. Knock.* This so-called evil that the old tales claim lives here is certainly not holding up at this very moment. So far, I've investigated almost the entirety of the castle, and haven't found a single piece of evidence to support that. I've found *nothing*. In my defeat, just as I turned to walk away, the black door squeaked. I spun around to catch it moving only another inch more. I held my candle out in front of me to illuminate whatever I could.

"Who's there?" I yelled, demanding an answer.

But there was no answer, only silence. I demanded again, asking who was in the room, but alas, not a peep. I took a step forward, extending my free hand as it touched the door. It was cold and damp from the humidity. My fingers felt sticky as I pushed the door in a little further, revealing more of the room. The candle sat still, melted almost down to the base, the small flame still dancing in the window. I glanced down at my feet as they brushed the threshold. I was afraid to cross over since I wasn't sure what person or thing awaited me on the other side. I took a deep breath, my candlestick still extended out in my hand as it entered the room before the rest of me.

The room was as muggy as the rest of the castle had been. The walls were black, with small, white-painted images across them. I made my way over to one of the walls to get a closer look at what the designs might be. I found enjoyment in the stories written about witches, warlocks, and fairies, and these shapes looked familiar. Some of them looked like stars, but they were upside down. Others looked like little people with sharp things growing out from all different angles of their bodies. There was one shape in particular that caught my eye. I took a step closer, placing my hand on top of it. It was the only shape drawn in a dark inky substance. It was the image of a girl. She was smiling, but one corner of her mouth drooped with uncertainty. Her hair appeared long enough that it reached her lower back, and a tattoo of a cat was sketched onto her arm. Wooden shapes were fastened together, suspended from the high ceiling above.

There were a few books stacked in the corner of the room on top of a red carpet with some sort of dark stain on it. There was even a pillow. It was used and honestly, pretty dirty. It looked as if someone had been staying here, or maybe even visiting daily. I walked over to the stack of books on the floor, leaning down closer to get a better look. I opened the first one on top, *A Ritual Guide*.

"Ritual?" I questioned, blowing some dust off of the plum-colored cover.

"I wouldn't touch any more of those," a voice whispered from behind me.

I turned around just as my candle went out. I stumbled to my feet and struggled to take a few steps back, the remenance of my candlestick falling to the floor with a *snap*. I reached for anything to help catch my balance but ended up on the floor, my legs spread over the stack of books.

"Stay away from me!" I yelled, at the top of my lungs. "I have a knife and I'll kill you!"

A masculine laugh sounded from the same area the voice had occurred seconds ago.

"I-I mean it!" I shouted again, trying to sound tough.

The owner of the voice was silent. Fearing for my life, I quickly made my way to my feet, brushing off the dust from my backside. I stepped to my left, escaping the corner of the room with the now-ruined stack of books.

I quickly walked over to the window and grabbed the tiny candle still aglow, "Who are you? I want to see your face!" I said, taking a deep breath in.

There was a snapping noise of sorts. Almost like someone snapped their fingers together and suddenly I saw a bright light. I covered my eyes with my arm and squinted when I opened them again. There was another candlestick lit, but this one was larger than the others. It was a tall, black candlestick and could defeat mine in a fight if it wanted to.

My eyes grew wide at the sight of him. It? Him? It was difficult to see in this lighting, but it had soft, brown hair that curled toward the ends. His eyebrows were darker than his hair, but not by much. It was taller than me, at least 3 feet taller. His eyes appeared as dark, gray, circles, hidden deep within his face, with a jaw that looked as if it could cut through stone. He wasn't smiling when he looked at me, but I could see the cold, purple-pink color of his lips. His head was tilted upward slightly, squinting his dark eyes, fixated in my direction. He almost didn't appear real. It was like I was stuck in a dream, fading in and out of sleep. Almost as if I were reading a book and I had gotten so lost in it that I began to daydream.

My heart fluttered rapidly with the same confusion that tangled my thoughts. I had never felt such an intense pounding in my chest before. The longer I stared, the more real he became. He flickered in and out of sight with the orange flame of the candle. My heart danced mysteriously inside my heavy chest.

He just stood there, staring at me, both of us breathing uneasily in the silence.

...

I wanted it known that he wouldn't keep me trapped here so I pushed my hand forward and held the candlestick closer to him.

"I'm going to leave now," I said, glancing toward the open door.

He chuckled, nodding in agreement, "That's fine by me. You're the one who broke in and disturbed me."

I gasped, "Disturbed *you?* You're not even supposed to be in here! This place has been abandoned for years. Not to mention how disgusting it is here."

He smiled, turning away as if he were hiding something, "I've been here for quite some time and each time someone breaks in, they end up destroying more and more."

My eyes scanned the room, "What are you doing in here anyway? Where's your family? Your friends?"

He nodded once more, "Ah yes, I haven't seen them since I was born. I was an orphan. Now that I think of it, I don't remember them at all."

I could feel my eyes grow heavy, speaking the only word that came to mind, "Oh."

"Being alone can be harmonious," he whispered.

I looked down at my shoes, remembering how long it was going to take me to get home. It was also hours past midnight. My nerves about him had faded in our conversation and when I glanced up to speak again, he was gone. It was as if I had been standing in this dark room alone the entire time.

"Hello?" I said, spinning around to check the entirety of the room.

But in the darkened silence, I was alone.

Dawn

The soft, morning sunlight coming in through the window warmed my face, waking me at 8:43 am. I rolled over, turning away from the light, rubbing the sleep from my eyes. I had only forgotten about the castle and the young man there for merely a moment before my memory sparked visions, reminding me of the night. My thoughts were jumbled trying to remember if he was real, or if it was just my imagination playing tricks on me. Part of me thought it could have been the castle, toying with my mind, or potentially, the lack of sleep. I stretched my arms far above my head and rubbed my feet together, creating warm, comforting friction. I hadn't been able to sleep, arriving home after only 3 a.m., careful not to wake anyone.

I swung my legs over the side of my bed, putting my favorite pair of fuzzy, pink slippers on, and headed down the stairs. I could hear my parents chatting, the smell of coffee and fresh breakfast in the air.

"Good Morning, Hun!" My mom said, sipping her steaming cup of coffee.

My dad was reading something on the table, but he looked up for a moment and smiled in my direction.

"I'm hungry," I said, eyeing the fresh waffles on the counter.

My dad cleared his throat, still looking down at whatever it was that had his attention, "Just made those if you want some! Bacon is on the way as well."

I opened the cabinet and grabbed a clean, glass plate, placing it down on the counter with a *clink*. The waffles smelt delicious, so I grabbed three and loaded them with maple sweet syrup.

I reached for a mug and began to pour myself a cup of coffee when I heard my mom laugh, "Coffee? You never drink that."

I shrugged, "I'm just tired today, so I need something to help me wake up."

She nodded in agreement, "Now you know why your father and I drink it every day!"

They both chuckled as I brought my food to the table. As I ate, my dad lifted the paper he had been reading. I glanced over to find a photo of the castle on the front page.

"What is that?" I asked, taking a bite out of the waffles, syrup running down the side of the fork.

"This?" My father asked, handing the paper over in my direction.

I put my fork down on the edge of the plate and took a closer look at the paper. I almost choked on my coffee after reading the words, *Abandoned Castle Becomes Hazardous Trespassing Playground.*

"What?" I squealed, practically making both my parents jump out of their skin.

I shook the paper and my head both at the same time, "Did they catch someone in there recently?"

My dad nodded, "I believe so."

My mom interrupted, "It's been sitting vacant for years, so it's probably about time they do something with it."

I felt a wave of guilt rising through me. I wasn't afraid of being caught; instead I was unsure of what to say, or how I was truly feeling. It's possible the feeling of guilt mingled with relief. I had visited for one night but felt an instant connection to the place.

My dad put his hands on the table, fingers intertwined, "It's probably not very safe. I'm sure they don't want kids breaking in anymore, destroying more than they already have." Then he shook his head. "They should just tear it down."

"What if someone wanted to buy it to fix it and live there? I think that would be a great idea," I said, standing up with my half-empty plate.

My parents glanced at one another, a twisted look spread across their faces. I emptied the remaining food into the trash, placing my plate in the sink.

"I'm going to go read for a while, out by the big oak," I explained, taking my coffee with me.

Morning Dew

    I slipped out the back door, my coffee and a book in hand, making my way out toward the oak. The grass underneath my feet was damp from the morning dew and the birds were singing cheerfully in the trees above. There was a gentle, cool breeze blowing, which was normal for the early fall weather. October was just beginning to creep around the corner, which meant the leaves were on their way to changing their colors. Some of the trees were already bright red and orange, and some shed a decent amount of their leaves. I've always found it funny how some leaves begin the decaying process before others. I guess it works the same with a lot of things in life.

    When I got to the oak tree, I drank the rest of my coffee, placing the mug at the bottom of it. I slipped the book under my armpit and began to climb. I got to the very top where one of the sturdy branches could hold my weight and took a deep breath. I settled in, leaning my back against the trunk of the tree and my legs stretched out in front of me. A few of the leaves on the branch had begun to change and I was able to see the castle more easily.

An hour went by as I read and pondered the birth of the castle. I wondered who had built it and why. I knew that each building had a story behind it. It was beautiful in the way that it was built for someone. It encapsulated their vision of a home and countless memories were then made within. Structurally, it was magnificent. It reminded me of something medieval as it stood, strong and proud just outside of the woods. If I had the means, I would buy it for myself. I could see myself sitting at the top of one of the peaks in the window, reading as the light came in. I would light candles each evening, allowing the castle to emit a powerful glow into the darkness of the night. I would put on the fanciest of dresses I could find and dance endlessly to the sound of a piano playing. I would admire the luscious, ever-changing landscape from high above, and adore the stars at midnight. I wonder if that man was caught trespassing last night. If so, the town could make plans to tear the castle down. He probably doesn't even know of the news about the destruction that may await in the future.

Maybe I should tell him.

…

I left my book on the branch of the oak tree, high above so that no one could see it. I figured it would be easier to grab it on the way back than to bring it inside the castle, fearing I would accidentally leave it behind. I returned to the stonewall and climbed over the way I had the night before. I entered through the broken window on the bottom level and hopped down to the wooden floor below. The castle looked different in the daylight. The wooden floors gleamed across the halls, covered in many broken and misplaced items. The walls were all painted with an assortment of colors, yet the paint was so old and damp that it peeled in layers. There were fireplaces in almost every room, except the kitchen. Bookshelves full of dusty books, and old, broken chairs were mainly the only furniture left behind. The deep, red carpet on the stairs was perishing from the rain that had leaked in through a hole in the roof above. It looked as though a tree had fallen on top of the castle roof at one time, creating a small hole that allowed further decay.

"Hello!" I yelled out, hoping to hear someone respond.

I stood on the stairs for a moment listening, but after hearing nothing in the silence, I began to ascend the stairs further. I was practically running up the stairs so fast that I tripped at the top step, catching myself with my hand. I stood up, rubbing my hand on the leg of my jeans. I felt a pinch and looked down, the blood pooling in my palm. I rolled my eyes and pressed it against the side of my leg once more, allowing the pressure to stop the bleeding. I took in a deep breath and peered down the hallway. It was eerily dark even in the daytime. It seemed as though the windows had been covered with something thick enough to hold the darkness in. It didn't help with the mold build-up either, because the scent was stronger than I had smelt it the previous night. I took a few steps down the hall, feeling the wall for a covered window. When I found one, I pulled at the blanket-type cloth that hung over it. After a few tugs, it let go and fell uneasily to the floor. The light beamed in, attacking the darkness forcefully. I pulled down two more blankets until I felt something touch my arm.

I jumped back, terrified of what was latching itself onto me. I stumbled to find my balance and looked in his direction.

"You practically gave me a heart attack!" I squealed, rubbing my arm with my hand.

He smiled, the bright white of his teeth showing faintly through his pink-purple lips, "What are you doing?"

"I-I thought it needed some light in here... It was dark," I said, pointing at the curtains now lying in the hall.

I noticed his eyes shifting from the hall back toward my hand, "What is that?"

I looked down, "What is what?"

"That," He said, pointing at my bloody palm.

The clothing he was wearing was quite interesting. I hadn't noticed it the night before because it was too dark to see clearly, but he was wearing all black. His legs were longer than I first thought, and his black shirt was covered with a long, black cloak. He stood at least 8 feet tall, so he was lucky the ceilings in this place could accommodate his height. I had never seen a human stand that tall before though, which caused a heavy feeling in my chest to grow.

He twisted his head slightly to the right and answered his own question, "Blood."

I choked on my words, "Ya, I fell coming up the stairs... I'm fine though."

He didn't walk like a normal human either, he seemed to saunter, "I could smell it."

My eyes grew wide, my cheeks red, "Smell it?"

He stood still for a moment, pointing down the hall behind me. I turned to see what he was pointing at, but when I turned back to face him, he had disappeared into the shadowy hall.

A Ritual Guide

I threw the books down on my bedroom floor: one was the book I had left in the oak and the other was *A Ritual Guide* I had stolen from the dark candle room in the castle. I didn't touch either for a moment, unsure of what I was getting myself into. I crouched down folding my legs underneath me and rubbed my fingers across the front cover. It was still dusty from sitting inside the castle and the pages felt damp. The cover was plain black without any design. It looked like something had been etched into the cover, but it was hard to tell what it said. Studying it closer, the letters began to look more like someone's initials. Whoever this book belonged to, they hadn't used it in quite some time, so I'm sure they won't mind me borrowing it for a little bit.

I flipped the cover open to the first page. It was soggy and dirty, covered in fingerprints. There were little designs drawn throughout the page, similar to those I saw drawn on the walls inside the dark candle room.. I began to read the words *ritual, demon,* and *satanic.* As I turned the pages, I noticed small stains that weren't fingerprints, but droplets of some sort. It almost looked like…

"*BLOOD!*" I yelled, pushing the book away and watching it slide across the floor.

I brought my trembling fingers to my lips with a gasp and peered around the room as if someone had seen me in this state of panic.

"What the *hell*?" I whispered to myself, realizing what kind of book I was now in possession of.

My entire body trembled as I wrapped my arms around my legs, bringing them close to my chest. So many questions had begun to stir in my brain: *What type of book is this? Who does this book belong to? What was it used for? What will happen to me since I stole it? Am I going to die? Is there a demon?*

The stories I was told as a child began to dance within my mind, blurring the questions. I took a deep breath in, crawling across the floor to retrieve the book again. *Was it true that the castle had hidden secrets? Was there something evil residing there? Did that person even know what kind of place he was staying in?*

I had to do something, anything.

Dougal

Back inside the castle, I carried the book tightly under my arm. I placed my hand on the railing of the stairs and started up toward the partial sunlight shining in from behind one of the curtains. I took a deep breath before continuing up the stairs to the dark candle room. Before I could even reach for the doorknob, it clicked open.

A voice spoke, "Welcome back, girl!"

I entered the room, cloaked in shadow with a single candle lit to free some of the darkness. I scrunch my face together, "My name is Elia and I'm here to talk."

He raised both of his arms, exposing long, pale fingers as his robe fell back, "Elia, it is a pleasure to make your acquaintance."

I half smiled, "Ya, so, do you have a name?"

He looked to the right side of the room and then back at me, "Why don't you give me one?"

My face froze, "You don't have one already?"

He shook his head, unknowingly lying, one of his brown curls dangling in front of his eye. "I've never been given a name."

Holding the book behind my back hoping he wouldn't notice, I sighed, "Ok, I think you look like a - Dougal."

"Dougal," he repeated.

I smiled, "Yes, that's perfect."

He moved about the floor in an odd, sweeping fashion, "Why did you choose Dougal?"

I tried to distract him with the name game we had going on, but he was still somehow looking at me without looking directly at me. I could constantly feel his eyes studying me closely, "In my readings, I've found that it means 'dark stranger,' which is exactly what you are."

"Dark stranger!" He chirped excitedly, "How intriguing!"

A dark stranger is exactly what you are. I felt my body tense at the sound of hearing it aloud, along with his acceptance of such a name. I stood still, a few feet away from him across the room, the book still clutched in my hand behind my back. I felt my cheeks growing red as his robe swept across the floor, an odd smile painted across his face. *He's accepted the name. He's a dark stranger. That's exactly what he is.*

"What is it that you have to hide there behind your back?" He asked, catching me completely off guard.

"Hm?" I questioned, trying to play stupid.

His brows furrowed, "That, there." He began to raise his left hand, his long, sharp fingernail pointing toward me.

"This?" I asked, raising the book I had stolen from the room.

He was silent, a look of anger and confusion spread across his face, "Where did you get that?"

My eyes found the corner of the room, "I only took it to read it because I'm a huge bookworm."

He licked his lips, his purple tongue making its presence known. I walked over to the corner of the room lightly, placing it down gently back on top of the other books.

He tilted his head, "Well, did you enjoy your reading?"

Flustered, words slipped out of my mouth, "I-I just wanted to read it."

It was as if I had been dreaming. One minute he was across the room from me, speaking of names and questioning me about the book, and the next, he was right beside me. I glanced up at his face peering down at me like an evil serpent. He reached down past me, his hand gliding across the cover of the book. The room fell silent.

I blinked and he was gone.

Cole

The room grew cold as I stood with my arms wrapped around myself. I glanced around the silent room, Dougal still missing. He vanished completely right before my own eyes. I took a deep breath, frozen in place with fear. It was at that moment I knew what I had gotten myself involved in. There was a demon in this castle and he has secrets that he now knows I've been revealing.

The silence remained as I gained the courage to turn toward the large, black door. I knew I needed to leave the room as fast as possible, and I was sure as hell ready to be free of this place. I stepped quietly, not sure of where Dougal could be. Just as my hand made contact with the doorknob, Dougal's long, black cloak swept over me and I let out a blood-curdling scream.

"Are you afraid?" He asked, my back still facing him.

I shivered, speaking toward the door, "I just need to get home."

The floor creaked, "Home?"

I nodded, turning myself around slowly, "Yes, I need to go home to my family. They're probably looking for me now anyway."

The floor creaked again, "But, why don't you stay a bit longer?".

"I could come with you," he said, his white teeth sparkling in the flickering candlelight.

"That's probably not a good idea," I said, shaking my head.

His face drooped, "We've built a friendship here."

I couldn't help but laugh at his words, "Friendship?"

He flew across the room, getting so close to my face I could feel the chill of his breath, "You think this is funny?"

I closed my eyes tightly, shaking my head, "No, no."

Aggressively he spoke, "Then why did you laugh?"

I felt the heat of anger building inside of me as I opened my eyes to challenge him, "You're a demon. You're dead, aren't you?"

The demon grew larger as he backed away from me. His cloak seemed to sweep the floor more heavily as his eyes grew into hollowed holes. His mouth began to gape wider than I ever imagined possible and it scared the hell out of me. I turned around, running for the door. It swung open with a *smash* against the wall on the other side and I tripped down the hallway while making my escape. I grabbed the railings on the staircase, the rain pelting my head as it fell from the rotted hole in the ceiling above. The old, musty, red carpet *sloshed* under my feet and soaked my shoes. I fell down the stairs due to my feet moving faster than the rest of me. I made my way toward the window when I heard a voice in the room next to me. It wasn't as deep as the Dougal's. It sounded more like a - *human.*

"RUN!" I screamed, lunging toward the window, my body spilling out on the other side.

I fell onto the crispy grass, my arm cracking under my weight. I heard the human voice again, but my state of panic made it impossible to hear what they were saying. I began to climb the brick wall when I realized I was injured. My arm was throbbing. I heard someone behind me and when I turned around, I saw Cole.

Cole. The boy I snuck out to meet when I was only 16.

The Secret Path

"Get off of me!" I yelled, trying to break Cole's grip on my arm.

"I'm trying to help you!" He boomed back, reminding me of why things didn't work out between us in the first place.

I sighed, the pain and panic causing me to shake, "We have to get out of here!"

He nodded, pointing toward the land around the back of the castle, "Ok, this way!"

He began to run as I followed close behind, holding my arm to my chest hoping the pain would soon reside. We made our way around the back of the castle where there was just enough light to see the gardens. They went on for miles, vast and overgrown. There was a statue of a figure standing in the middle as if it were overlooking the grounds, but the vines were already overtaking its monstrous sight. It was difficult to recognize when we finally left the castle's land and entered the forest itself. The trees moaned in the breeze and I felt a chill run up my spine. I did my best to keep my eyes on Cole's back, watching him turn around every minute or so to check on me. We made it to a clearing where he must have known we were far enough away before slowing down.

I fell to the harsh, forest floor with a thud. It almost felt as if I were falling asleep, but I kept waking to Cole shaking me. I couldn't hear what he was saying due to the severe pain resonating from my arm. I blinked once or twice before taking a deep breath and then I don't remember absolutely anything.

…

I was running across a field of tall, green grass. Wildflowers had begun to fill the empty spaces and the summertime bugs buzzed with delight. The sun had just begun to set; a soft orange glow spread amongst the vast field. My feet swept gently against the earth as the dirt grew caked against the bottoms of my feet. I felt such freedom without shoes. The air was warm --- a slight breeze taking my breath away as it raced by my sides. I turned my head up to the sky, smiling. The puffy, white clouds raced along with me, high above the field. BEEP. As I slowed, I began to spin. The music played faster and faster as I spun, round and round. BEEP. I would run through the lush green forests. I would dance in the rain during a thunderstorm and catch the raindrops on my tongue. BEEP. I would climb the tallest tree to watch the sunset peacefully in the valley. I would spend my mornings in the gardens, smelling the sweet scents of flowers, and watching the bees work joyfully. I could see Cole, walking down the dirt path in the rain. He had a tall umbrella to catch the cool drops, but he was smiling. BEEP. The natural world is such a beautiful place in my mind. I wish I could stay here forever. BEEP.

...

One would think that after enduring so much pain and running through the woods at night from a demon you might sleep for ages, but for me, that wasn't the case. I jolted awake in my hospital bed, tearing at my chest with my good arm, gasping for air. The heart monitor began to beep faster and faster as nurses rushed into the room. My mother was asleep on the chair across from my bed before I just scared her almost to death. The nurses calmed me down, using deep breathing techniques and checking all my IV levels.

"She's ok," the doctor said to my mother, whose wild hair made it look like he had just gone through a wind tunnel.

They both stared at me for a minute before my mother whispered something back to the doctor. He nodded, looking down at his clipboard. He turned to smile at me and walked out of the room, leaving only my mother and I.

She came over to the side of the bed, "Hey, sweetie, how are you feeling?"

I half smiled, "I'm ok - just some arm pain."

She nodded, "I mean, you did a pretty good job almost breaking it."

Wide-eyed, I looked down at my arm, "What?"

My mother sighed, leaning against the hospital bed, "Your wrist is sprained. How did this even happen?"

I looked around the room, unsure of what to say, "I tripped."

She scrunched her face, confused, "Tripped? Where?"

"I - I was with a friend and we were running and I just fell," I said, stumbling over my words.

"Mhm," she said, nodding, "Well, when you want to tell me the truth, I'll be here!"

I coughed, "OK, I was with my friend Cole...well, he's not my friend."

My mom sat up straight, "Is Cole your boyfriend?"

I shook my head, "Uh, no. We went to school together."

She leaned forward, rubbing my hand, "You know we can talk about these types of things. I want you to know you can open up to me."

I smiled, "I know Mom, and I love you for that, but really, he's just my friend."

She nodded, staring into my eyes, "I love you too, but you need to be more careful."

I nodded in agreement, still thinking about what I had just experienced back at the castle.

My mom stood, stretching her legs, asking if I wanted something to eat but I was too lost in my thoughts, "Wait, mom, how did I even get here?"

I moaned in pain as I held myself up on my side, sure not to bump my wrist. There were moments when the shock almost made me black out again as I closed my eyes, but I knew I needed to be strong. I needed to know how I even got to the hospital.

The doctor came into the room with a nurse at his side, "Ready to go kiddo?"

Kiddo. Really? This guy doesn't know I'm older than 15.

I nodded, "Yep, and my mom should be back any minute. I think she went to get something to eat."

He smiled, "We already caught her in the hallway and she said to get you ready for when she comes back."

…

On the car ride home, I found myself silent, staring out the window at the landscape. I didn't want to tell my mom exactly what happened, but I knew Cole had something to do with all of this. He's a puzzle piece to the chaos.

"Hey, Mom, I still want to know how I got to the hospital," I said, my eyes still staring straight ahead.

She sighed, "Well, they said a boy carried you into the emergency room claiming that you passed out from an injury."

My eyes went wide as I looked over at her, "What?"

She nodded, "Mhm and I'm thankful he brought you in when he did."

I smiled, "Me too because this sucks."

My mom let out a laugh, "Just wait until your father sees all of this."

I sighed, "I don't even want to think about it."

We sat in silence for the remainder of the ride home and I'm thankful we did. The pain was subsiding and the medicine they gave me was beginning to lull me to sleep.

Hours

I awoke in my bed to a tapping noise outside my window. *Tap. Tap. Tap.* The medicine the doctor had given me put me to sleep on the car ride home and I felt as though I'd been asleep for weeks. Dusk was just entering the world as I rubbed my sleepy eyes, unsure of what time it was. I heard the tapping a few more times, *tap, tap, tap.* My bedroom was on the second floor of the house, so other than an animal or the rain, I'm not sure anyone could climb to this height. I rolled over and tried to ignore the tapping, deciding it was probably a bird.

Tap. Tap. Tap.

I groaned, "Who is it?"

Of course, there was no answer. I groaned again and rolled out of bed onto my feet. I stood up, holding my wrist, and walked over to the window. I peered through the shades and noticed a figure standing in the grass below. I felt the sudden urge to puke. The nausea was either the medicine, the pain from my wrist, the demon I saw, or the fact that a stranger was standing under my window. I rubbed my eyes and squinted to get a better look. The figure looked like a human and resembled…Cole. *COLE.*

I lifted the shades and opened my window, "What are you doing here? How do you even know where I live?"

"Good questions!" He yelled.

I shushed him, trying to keep him quiet, "Shhh! My parents are here and if they hear you, they may suspect something."

He lowered his voice, "Suspect something? What does that even mean?"

I rolled my eyes and sighed, "How do you even know where I live?"

I couldn't see his face very well, but I had a feeling he was smiling, "I asked Jennifer."

Jennifer. The girl who snuck out with me when we were just kids. Oh, and of course Cole is the boy we snuck out to see.

I nodded, "Ahhh, that makes sense. So, what are you doing here again?"

He began speaking louder, "Can you just come down here and talk to me so I don't have to keep yelling and alert your parents that a guy is standing in the backyard?"

I shushed him again, "OK, stop. I'll come down. Just give me a second."

I shut the window carefully and turned toward my bed. I was wearing a bathrobe, but it would have to do. I don't even think I could get myself dressed with my wrist throbbing, let alone this annoying wrap on it.

I made my way down the stairs, looking around for my parents. I heard a TV on in the living room so I snuck around into the dining room and out the side door near the garage. Although I'm 21, I still don't like to tell my parents a lot about my life. They seem to care too much about who I'm with or what I'm doing when it comes to a guy. Cole was standing by a tree in the backyard, kicking something around with his feet.

"Hi," I said, trying not to show my nervous smile.

"How's the wrist?" He asked, pointing toward the wrap, half falling off.

I shrugged as if I wasn't phased by the throbbing pain, "It's fine. I'll be fine."

He smiled and looked down at his feet, "Ok, that's good. So, about what happened…"

I cut him off before he could finish his thought, "I don't want to talk about it."

His eyes met mine, "But we should. I'm still confused about why you were running out of that place like the devil was after you."

I gave him a disgusted look, "Is that supposed to be funny? I nearly died."

He smiled, "It is kind of funny. But, what do you mean *nearly died?* The fall wasn't that bad. You only hurt your wrist."

I laughed as if I couldn't believe what I was hearing, "I *nearly died* because of that thing! That demon thing!"

Cole's eyes widened and his face grew pale. It was so pale I could see it in the dark.

Concerned by his facial expression, I asked, "Are you ok?"

He coughed as he ran his fingers through his sandy blonde hair, looking around, "Uh, ya, I'm alright. I'm just confused by the word *demon.* Like you think you saw a…"

I cut him off again, "*Think?* No. I don't *think* I saw anything. I *know* what I saw and what I saw was not human."

Cole shuffled in place and laughed, "Those drugs they have you on are doing something to your imagination."

I was shocked. I couldn't believe what I was hearing. Does he think this is a joke? He thinks I would just make all of this up and have jumped out a window and broken a bone for nothing? I turned around and began walking back toward my house.

Cole reached out and grabbed my arm, "Wait," he said, "I believe you."

I shrugged him off, "I'm not joking around. I saw someone or something in there. I spoke to it."

Cole looked at me in disbelief, "Spoke to it? What do you mean?"

I nodded, "I went in there the other night and he spoke to me like he was a normal person. It looked like he had been living there."

"Like a homeless person?" Cole asked.

I shook my head, "No, not like a homeless person. He was tall, like 8 feet tall, and he was dressed in all black."

Cole sniffed, "I'm sure it was just some homeless dude being creepy. Don't go back there alone."

I smirked, "It was not some *homeless dude*. It was a demon."

He shook his head as if what I was saying didn't mean anything, "Well anyways, you're welcome for saving you and all that heroic stuff."

I tried to hide my smile, disguised by annoyance in my voice, "I'm fine, but thanks for helping me out of there even though I don't remember any of it."

He nodded, "Anytime."

We both stood in the dark, silent and cold from the late September breeze. I shifted around on my feet, unsure of what to say next.

Before I could speak, Cole interrupted my thoughts, "Well, I'm going to head home. I'm glad you're ok. I'll come check on you tomorrow."

I was thankful for the cover of darkness because I'm pretty sure I was blushing, "You don't have to do that. I'll be fine."

"Sure," he said, "Until that demon comes to get you."

"Shut up," I said, nudging him with my good hand.

He laughed, "Goodnight, and don't let the demons bite."

Oddly enough, I began to laugh as I turned and walked back toward the door, "Whatever you say, Cole."

I watched him walk away through the crack in my door. He walked toward a street lamp on the road, his long black pants sweeping against the dirt as he walked.

Jennifer

After Cole left, I quietly snuck back into my room. I texted Jennifer to ask her about Cole and why she told him where I lived. She replied, *Well, he seemed genuinely concerned and wouldn't tell me what happened so I just told him. IDK.*

I rolled my eyes and told her it was fine, but that he showed up outside my house. Not to mention it was a bit strange that he knew which window was mine.

She seemed puzzled. *How would he know which window was yours? That's weird.*

I told her I also thought it was weird, but next time I see him I'll check it out. She knows I'm not afraid to ask. I asked her if she was busy and she replied, *Nah. I've got nothing going on. Wanna hang tomorrow?*

I was so thankful she was free because I needed to vent and she always made me feel better.

...

The next day, Jennifer showed up at my door around 10 in the morning. She had a huge smile pasted on her face and lunged at me for a hug.

"Be careful of my wrist!" I shouted, startling her enough to let go.

"Oh my gosh, I'm so sorry. I already forgot," she said, stumbling back and reaching her hands out toward me.

I laughed, "It's fine. I was just getting myself ready when you showed up."

She smiled, "Do you need help with anything since your wrist is ya know, damaged and all?"

I shrugged, "Not really, but it's not easy putting clothes on."

She giggled, "Ya I bet."

I smiled, "So, do you want to grab a coffee or something? I haven't had any today and I feel like a zombie."

She nodded, "Uh, duh. I'll never say *no* to a cup of coffee."

I laughed, "I didn't think so. Where do you want to go?"

She looked around the room, "Uh, do you want to check out that new place, *Coffee Breaks with Bri*? I heard their coffee is delicious."

I nodded, "Ya, let me just go grab my sweatshirt and we can go."

Jennifer jumped in the air and squealed, "Ahh, I'm beyond excited. I'll go start my car!"

Making my way up the stairs I yelled back, "Ok, I'll meet you out there!"

…

We pulled into the parking lot in Jennifer's green BMW. It was a nice car, but I already missed driving mine. I had a red Subaru WRX and I was honestly pretty sad about not being able to drive it around for the next few weeks. I needed my wrist to heal fully before I got back on the road alone. Jennifer parked and we both got out.

"Ok, this place is adorable," she shrieked, clasping both of her hands together.

I laughed, "It already looks like they make good coffee just from the outside."

Jennifer smiled as she opened the door for me, "I've heard it's the best. What are you going to get?"

I shrugged, thanking her for getting the door, "I'm not sure yet."

We walked inside and there was a small line of people standing at the counter. The lights were bright in the front section, but the back of the place looked different. Studying the layout, it looked like your typical cozy coffee shop, but there was a specific section toward the back that looked like it had 3 bookshelves full of books. The ambiance of the place, with its inviting chairs, soft music, and walls adorned with art, and books stacked to the ceiling, promised a haven away from the hustle and bustle of daily life.

"Hey, can we get our coffee and sit back there?" I asked, pointing toward the bookshelf room.

Jennifer nodded, "Of course."

When it was our turn, Jennifer ordered a coffee that had extra ice and whipped cream that looked like it was going to touch the ceiling. There were little pieces of chocolate on the top and chocolate swirl inside the plastic cup itself. I ordered something called a *Banana Pistachio Brew*. It sounded like something I'd enjoy, so I gave it a try.

After we paid, we walked toward the section of the coffee shop with the bookshelves. They were so tall that they touched the ceiling. We sat down at an empty table in the corner and Jennifer started talking. I couldn't hear what she was saying because I was mesmerized by the amount of books this place had. There were different genres labeled in each section and each one was jam-packed full.

"Elia, are you listening to me?" Jennifer said, piercing through my daydream and breaking the trance I was in.

Apologetically, I looked in her direction, "What?"

She shook her head, smiling softly, "You looked lost for a minute. Are you ok?"

I nodded, "Oh, I'm fine. I was just looking at all the books around here."

Jennifer laughed calmly, "You've always been a bookworm."

I nodded back in agreement, changing the subject of the conversation, "How's your coffee? It looks fancy."

She looked down at her coffee and slowly spun it around a few times, "It's delicious. It's called a *Mocha Chocolate Chip.*"

My eyes widened with surprise, "Wow, that sounds good. I ordered a *Banana Pistachio Brew.*"

Jennifer made a funny face, "That sounds… interesting. How does it taste?"

My coffee was fairly simple compared to her order, but I sipped it quickly and exclaimed, "It's incredible!"

She smiled happily, "Now we know where to come when we want coffee."

I looked around the room at the people sipping their coffees, munching on pastries, and reading the different books this place had to share. There was a young girl with a book in her hand that had a star on the binding. She looked to be about the same age as Jennifer and I, maybe even a little older, around 26. She wore a long purple dress that hung past her ankles, a garment that seemed to capture the essence of elegance. It was a deep purple, the kind that reminded onlookers of twilight skies just before the stars made their grand appearance. The small flowers embroidered on the fabric seemed to come alive, dancing around her feet like delicate sprites celebrating the moon's rise. The way the material caught the light and the shadows played among the folds added a mysterious allure, making her presence not just seen but felt. I squinted my eyes and turned my head, trying to get a better look at the title of the book she was reading. It looked as if it said something like *Witches, Warlocks, and How to Cast Spells*. During my investigation of the book title, she glanced over at me. She gave me a half smile, indicating she was a little weirded out by my staring. Uncomfortable from being caught, I smiled back and took another sip of my coffee.

I nudged Jennifer who was staring off into the distance behind me, "Do you see that book over there? That looks like a good one."

But Jennifer didn't move, nor did she even respond. She kept staring past me like she had seen a ghost.

I turned around to face the direction she was looking and saw a guy with blond hair standing at the counter. He was wearing a dark blue hoodie and a pair of black pants. His boots were caked in mud.

My brain went through a variety of names before I landed on the one I wanted to say, "Cole."

Jennifer reached across the table and grabbed my wrist, making me jump as I turned back to face her, "Well, this is kind of awkward."

The Girl in the Purple Dress

Jennifer had this comical-looking grin on her face like she was about to get on stage and say something funny enough to perform for a crowd. I felt my eyes twitch, staring at her with my, *do not say anything weird, uncomfortable, or embarrassing* face. While we were looking into the souls of one another, I felt a cool breeze pass by my side and I glanced over to see Cole now sitting with the girl in the purple dress.

"How did he not notice us?" Jennifer whispered, giggling to herself with unease.

"I don't know. Who is that girl?" I rolled my eyes and felt my grasp tighten around my coffee.

Jennifer's expression changed just then. Her comical-looking face changed into a face of slow-growing confusion. "Wait a minute, are you into him?"

I choked on my coffee, coughing quietly and shaking my head in response to her. "No, I'm not *into* him. I've just never seen that girl before. She doesn't look familiar."

Jennifer began to smile, "Look, Elia, I want to believe you but I'm finding it hard when your face is pink and there are beads of sweat rolling down your forehead."

I reached across the table and nudged her gently, "Stop. I'm being serious."

"Alright, I believe you," Jennifer said, rubbing her arm where my hand had just made contact. "But, I'm not sure who she is. I like her dress though."

Just as I was about to say something, I began to get the feeling as if someone were staring at me. I felt like something was making its way up my neck, crawling slowly and eerily. It reminded me of the feeling I had in the castle with that *thing*. The feeling I had with Dougal, the dark, monstrous, evil-looking *thing*. I took a deep breath in before looking over at the table where the girl in the purple dress had been sitting. Cole was sitting with her, but this time they were both looking directly at me. Instead of smiling, she was making a face full of shock and disgust. Her eyebrows furrowed, yet her eyes were the size of golf balls. Her dress began to change color. It was no longer this beautiful purple, but rather a deepening red. Uncomfortable and panicked, I grabbed hold of my coffee, stood up, and began walking toward the door. I heard Jennifer saying something behind me and the sound of a chair being scraped across the floor. I didn't turn around though. I just kept walking until I made it outside.

"What the hell are you doing?" Jennifer shouted, running out the door behind me, coffee still in hand.

"Let's go home," I said, pulling on the door handle nervously and getting into the passenger seat of her car.

She stood outside the car for a minute before opening the door and climbing in, "What's going on?"

"Nothing," I said, buckling myself in with the seatbelt.

"That wasn't *nothing* Elia. That was something." Jennifer said, starting the car and backing out of the parking spot.

I rubbed the back of my neck, "I'll explain it when we get back to my house."

Jennifer didn't say anything. She just backed out of the parking spot and began to drive. I glanced over at the window of the coffee shop, wondering what it was I had just seen. I stared out the window the entire drive home and Jennifer didn't say another word.

…

We pulled into the driveway and got out of the car. I unlocked the front door and we walked in, kicking our shoes off on the floor mat. I went to the kitchen and poured two glasses of water because I knew we would need them with the conversation we were about to have.

"Let's go up to my room," I said, still holding both glasses of water in each hand.

"Not until you tell me what's going on." Jennifer angrily snapped.

I looked at her in disbelief, "I am going to tell you what's going on, but I need to make sure we're safe and alone."

She looked confused, as she should be. This whole situation was confusing and quite unrealistic unless you believe in evil demons and heartache.

When we got to my room, I put the glasses of water down and closed the door behind us. I made sure to lock it just in case someone were to come into the house. I was feeling more paranoid than anything, but I needed to tell Jennifer about everything that had happened.

"Ok, so what's the deal? I'm confused." She said, looking genuinely concerned.

I moved uneasily on the floor, wrapping my arms around my legs, "There's a lot to tell you but I don't want you to freak out or anything."

Her eyes widened, "Freak out? Elia, you're scaring me."

I suddenly had the urge to puke, but I swallowed it down as I began to speak. I told her about the castle, about what I had seen and heard. I told her about Dougal and described him or *it* as best I could. I told her about the dirty old room and the satanic books I found. I mentioned how I took one home and regretted it once I realized what it was all about. I told her about Cole, the truth about how I hurt my wrist, and how Cole saved me that night. I also mentioned how he came to my window asking to talk. The whole time I was explaining everything, Jennifer just stared at me with her mouth wide open, tears pooling in her eyes. I knew she was uncomfortable, but I was just as uncomfortable talking about the experience. I felt as if I were trapped in some type of fairytale, but not that kind with a happy ending. This one was dark and ended in tragedy.

Tears

My bed was the only comfort I felt after speaking with Jennifer. I was thankful that I could just lay down and relax. Jennifer had cried after I told her about what I had been experiencing lately. She held onto me and cried. I don't think she was crying because she felt bad for me, I think she was crying because she was scared for me. I remember telling her it was fine and that I would figure out what was going on, but the look of horror in her eyes when I told her was still haunting me. I hope I didn't make a mistake.

Lost in my thoughts about Jennifer and the conversation we had, I suddenly heard a tapping noise at my window.

Tap. Tap. Tap.

I sighed and picked up my phone, texting Cole. *I know it was weird earlier at the coffee shop, but I'm not interested in talking to you right now.*

He replied almost immediately, *What are you talking about?*

Annoyed, I replied, *Just go home and we can talk about everything tomorrow or whatever. I'm tired.*

Suddenly, my phone began to ring from an incoming call. I rolled my eyes and answered, "Cole, just go home and we can talk tomorrow."

His voice was low and he sounded confused, "I called you because I don't understand what you mean by *go home*. I am home."

I looked at my window, listening again for the tapping, "Wait, you're not outside my window throwing rocks again?"

"Uh, no. Elia, I'm at home," he said, sounding concerned.

My breathing began to grow heavy and I felt that eerie feeling crawling up my neck, "Cole, someone is throwing rocks at my window."

"Well go check it out," he said, "Maybe it's Jennifer or something."

I moved my feet to the floor and slowly made my way over to the window, turning my lamp off as I passed by, "I don't think it's Jennifer."

He cleared his throat, "Who would it be then if it's not me or her?"

I shook my head as I began to peek out into the backyard, "I'm not sure."

There was a moment of silence before Cole asked again, "Who is it?"

The darkness stretched across the backyard, swallowing the moonlight and casting an uncomfortable paleness over everything it touched. My hands began to shake, my fingers trembling as if trying to escape the overwhelming sense of dread that consumed me. Tears welled in my eyes, blurring the already distorted scene before me. I felt my phone slip from my loosening grip, crashing to the ground, Cole yelling on the other end of the call. It wasn't just an absence of light; it was a presence, a tangible entity that seemed to pulsate with malevolence.

I choked on the thick air, each breath a struggle against the suffocating weight of fear pressing down on my chest. It felt like the oxygen itself had turned against me. I couldn't believe what I was seeing.

There he was. His monstrous shadow loomed in the darkness. How could he be here… standing in my backyard? It defied logic, challenged reason, and instilled the instinct to flee, to run far away from whatever unholy thing cast such a sinister presence.

But even as my instincts screamed for escape, I found myself rooted to the spot, unable to tear my gaze away from the darkness that seemed to reach out for me.

The sound of Cole screaming could still be heard as my cell phone lay on my bedroom floor. I stood at the window, frozen in place, staring at his looming presence next to the giant white oak tree. I wanted to look away, but the darkness of his being against the night sky consumed me.

Dougal lifted an arm and began to move it back and forth as if he were waving to me. I knew he could see me even in my room with the lights off because he was looking directly at me. It felt as if he were standing in the room with me, his hands touching my shoulders ever so lightly. The pressure on my chest grew deeper and deeper as I stood at the window watching him move his arm in a waving motion. I didn't know if I should wave back and acknowledge his existence or simply melt into the floorboards.

Just as I began to lift my arm to wave back, a hand wrapped around my mouth and pulled me onto the floor, out of sight of Dougal.

I struggled with the hand on my mouth and somehow managed to break out of the grip before turning around and swinging my arm at whoever it was. The darkness in my room had grown so murky that I couldn't see anything without the help of a light.

I screamed, urging the horror to retreat as I yelled, "Get away from me!"

Within the pitch-black room, I heard a familiar voice, "Elia, it's me."

Cole.

Without another thought, I lunged in the direction of his voice, the only comforting thing I felt at that moment.

He shushed me as I struggled to breathe and whispered, "Don't make a sound."

There was a strange noise outside my window just then. It sounded as if someone were scraping their fingernails on a chalkboard.

Cole whispered, "Light a candle and get under the bed, now."

"What?" I whispered back, "Why?"

I could hear the sound of Cole's heart thumping, "Because he's trying to get through the window and he won't be able to see us if we're hidden."

I did as Cole said, feeling around the room for a lighter. Luckily, I had a vanilla-scented candle on my dresser so I lit it and quickly crawled under the bed, pulling a blanket down on top of us.

The scraping noise stopped and I covered my mouth with my hand, Cole's arm wrapped around my side.

A terrifying voice spoke out, almost as if hissing the words in anger, "You can't hide Elia forever!"

I turned toward Cole in the darkness, tears streaming down my face, my hand still covering my mouth to quiet my breathing. I couldn't see Cole's eyes, but I knew he was there, staring back at me in horror.

Confession

The sunlight pierced through the window and illuminated the room with elegance. I opened my eyes to see Cole lying next to me, covered in a blanket, still under my dusty bed. He looked peaceful lying there, lightly breathing with the sunlight making his blonde hair shimmer. He looked almost angelic.

He began to moan as he stretched his arms and legs, cramped from sleeping in such an uncomfortable position, "Where am I?"

I didn't answer his question, but instead demanded an immediate answer, "Who are you, really?"

He squinted his eyes, looking at me with an odd expression, "What?"

I nudged him to move and rolled out from under my bed, checking the window to ensure we were alone, "I said, who the hell are you?"

He rubbed his eye, "Are you feeling ok? You're acting weird."

I almost couldn't believe he was speaking to me with a sense of humor. As if anything we went through last night was funny, "Don't play games with me. What the hell is going on? I want answers, now!" I shouted.

His face changed from a comical grin to a look of guilt, "I can try to explain what's going on, but seriously, it's just me, Cole."

I shook my head in anger, "I don't know if I can believe a word that comes out of your mouth. That *thing*! Dougal! He spoke to *you* last night. He spoke *directly to you!*"

Cole looked around the room, his expression changing with each thought that passed through his mind, "Dougal? Who is that?"

I stared at him, pointing my finger in the direction of my window, *"That dark, evil, monstrous, satanic, demon thing!"*

Cole turned his head, eyes glued to the window, "You gave it a name?"

My face must have been redder than blood, "Why did it speak to you? Almost like it knows you!"

Cole shook his head, "Elia, there's a lot you don't know and I don't think you want to know."

I began to cry, "I'm being haunted by this evil thing that I accidentally stumbled upon while exploring the castle and you think I don't want to know *why* and *how?* Cole, you knew how to hide from it and it spoke directly to *you* last night."

Cole scratched his head, his eyes now on mine, "I'll explain everything over a cup of coffee."

…

We drove to the coffee shop, but after we ordered, we went out to sit in the car. Cole sipped his coffee a few times before he spoke.

"I'm so sorry, Elia," he said, his hands trembling.

I shook my head, confused, "Sorry about what?"

He looked at me, his eyes a deep blue, "I'm so sorry you're involved now."

I squinted at him, "Involved in what exactly?"

He shook his head and sighed, "In this evil that you've named. What was it again? Dougal?"

I took a sip of my coffee and kept my gaze on Cole, "I named it Dougal because when I met it, I was horrified and thought that by giving it a name, maybe I'd feel some type of comfort."

Cole seemed to let out a type of half laugh, half sigh, "Well, Dougal was an accident."

I tilted my head, unsure of how to respond. Cole must have read my expression because before I could think of anything to say, he blurted out, "I did it. I made him, but it was an accident I swear!"

I sat back in the passenger seat of his car, sickened by his words. I felt as if I were going to puke remembering the candle that was lit in the castle window, the books in that dirty old room, and how I saw Cole when I ran from it. When I ran from Dougal.

I took another sip of my coffee, breathing heavily and shaking my head, "You made him, as in, you made a demon?"

Cole put his coffee in the cup holder, reaching his hand toward me, "It was an accident. I met this girl a few months back and she seemed really cool at first, but I started to notice that she had these weird little interests. Like, she liked reading about witches and spells and stuff. I didn't think it was weird until she actually started trying to cast spells…"

Before he could keep talking, I cut him off, "Wait, were you with her the other day, here? Was she the girl in the purple dress?"

He gulped, "Yes, that was Seraphina."

I shook my head, "Seraphina?"

He nodded quickly, "Ya, that's her. She's cool, but she likes to cast spells and do all this weird magic stuff that I thought was cool at first but after we made…"

I cut him off, "After you made Dougal, you regret getting to know her."

He nodded, his eyes now in his lap, "I don't know what the hell to do now."

I took a deep breath, "OK, well did you try talking to her about it? Maybe she can help get rid of him and bring him back to wherever he came from."

Cole chuckled this time, "You don't understand. Seraphina is a nice person, but you don't want to tell her *how, when, or why* she should do something. She can get really…"

"Dark," I blurted out before he had the chance.

He looked up at me, "Ya, dark."

We sat in silence, a thick tension hanging between us like a shroud of mystery. Cole, with his unwavering gaze, held me in a trance. Despite our long history as friends, there was an unsettling air of unfamiliarity about him at that moment.

In our high school days, Cole was rebellious. He was the guy hanging out at the skatepark, his laughter mingling with the smoke of his cigarettes. His weekends were a blur of recklessness featuring alcohol and adrenaline. Dressed in perpetual darkness, he seemed to embody the very essence of the night.

Yet, beneath that facade of defiance, there lurked a concern that felt almost palpable. A concern not just for my well-being, but perhaps for his own soul too. His piercing blue eyes held depths I could never hope to fathom, windows to a world of secrets and shadows.

Cole was a paradox, a contradiction wrapped in layers of darkness and light. He exuded an aura of danger, yet beneath it lay a vulnerability that called out to me, drawing me closer despite the warning bells ringing in my mind.

He was the kind of person you crossed the street to avoid, yet I found myself undoubtedly drawn to him, captivated by his presence. For in his eyes, I saw a reflection of my own inner unrest, a shared understanding.

As the world faded around us, I realized that Cole was not just a friend, but a kindred spirit bound to me by threads of fate and destiny. And as we sat in silence, I knew that our journey together was only just beginning.

In that moment, as our eyes locked onto each other, I knew we would do anything to rescue each other from this madness.

The Plan

I dug through my closet like a furious beast, looking for a bag big enough to fit an army.

"We should get going soon. It's almost dark," Cole said, kicking a cat toy around my room.

I glanced in his direction, still rummaging through my closet, "Give me a second, it's not like Seraphina is going to leave. She knows you're coming."

Cole sighed, "Well she might if she gets pissed off."

I laughed, "Pissed off at *you*? She'd probably rather suck face."

I heard Cole chuckle, "Suck face?"

My cheeks began to heat with embarrassment for speaking my thoughts aloud, "Obviously you guys are into one another. It's not a big secret."

I stared into the back of my open closet, pulling out a large blue bag. Cole was standing silently near the window now, but he wasn't looking outside. Cole's gaze was fixed directly on me. His eyes followed my figure as I stood up, tossing my bag onto the bed. I took a deep breath as he began to walk toward me, still no sound spewing from his lips. The room fell silent as he made his slow approach and I felt a strange sensation growing in my stomach. I felt as if I were going to puke, yet the boiling of my insides was almost calming despite what I had been going through. Cole stopped in front of me, his eyes still locked on mine. He reached his hand forward, touching my arm softly. I felt his breath on my face, cooling my now burning, red cheeks. I turned my eyes toward his hand as I took in the gentle sensation of his skin against mine.

Cole cleared his throat, breaking the silence, "We, uh, need to go soon. Get ready."

I didn't look at his face, but still stared at the space on my arm where his hand was just moments ago. My pale skin tingled as if a million tiny needles had pierced it, yet it was an enormous feeling of peace. His skin against mine was pure tranquility.

…

Cole turned his flashlight on and reached into his bag for another one, handing it to me with force, "Here, you'll need this to see where we're going."

The flashlight clicked as it turned on, illuminating the dark forest ahead. I turned it slightly to see Cole, who was smiling an uncomfortable smile back at me.

I nodded, "The plan is to *not* die, right?"

I heard Cole breathe in before letting out a small bit of laughter, "That's been the plan my whole life, Elia, you don't have to remind me."

I smiled into the night beyond us, "I guess that's not really a bad plan considering the circumstances."

"The circumstances of my life, ya," Cole replied, scanning the forest with his flashlight.

We walked for what seemed like hours before reaching the oak tree. The oak was tall and strong. It held so many wonderful memories for me. It was and still is the peaceful place I loved to read on warm, sunny days.

My thoughts were interrupted as Cole began to speak, whispering quietly, "She said she would meet me just outside the gates of the Castle."

I nodded, although I knew he couldn't see me agreeing with his statement, "And I'm going to hide behind that small gargoyle statue in the front near the trail, right?"

He pointed the flashlight under his chin, creating a shadow on his face against the bright, yellow light, "Yes, you wait by the gargoyle statue and do not let her see you. She doesn't know you're coming."

Confused, I shined the flashlight under my chin, illuminating my annoyance, "She doesn't know I'm coming?"

He shook his head, his shadow creating movement amongst the branches of the tree above, "I didn't mention it because I wasn't sure if she would come knowing you're part of this."

I turned my flashlight off, taking in the ghastly night surrounding us. Why would Cole keep me a secret from her? I was unwillingly now part of this too, and there had to be something greater for me to do rather than hide and look weak in comparison to Seraphina and that demonic creature she created. She's the reason it's even here in the first place. She's the reason I've been going through hell. She's the reason *for* this hell!

Cole interrupted my thoughts as he shined the flashlight at me, piercing my eyes and practically blinding me, "Elia, let's go. You know the plan. You hide behind the statue and I'll meet with her to talk. I'll tell her we need to get rid of the dark entity her and I created."

I nodded, looking down at the ground, "I'll hide and do nothing but appear weak and stupid."

Frustrated, Cole leaned against the trunk of the tree, "Elia, you're not weak or stupid. I just don't want you to get hurt."

"Get hurt?" I blurted out, angered by his nonchalant answer as to my whole role in all of this.

"Yes, get hurt!" Cole began to shout, "Dougal seems to be drawn to you. Who knows what it may do if you're inside the castle when she and I call out to it."

I felt myself shaking with anger and embarrassment as I replied, "Call out to it? That's an interesting way to say "*summon a demon.*"

I could tell Cole was growing more and more upset with me as each moment passed, "Please, Elia, just follow the plan. I don't want you to get hurt. You're important to me."

I let out a laugh of pure exasperation, my flashlight still turned off, "What's important to you is being the hero, but it's fine. Let's just get this over with so I can get back to my normal life."

Cole sighed, "Elia, I'm doing this *for you*. Now, please, turn your flashlight back on and follow me."

I'm not sure why I obeyed his orders, but I was already beginning to feel the exhaustion crawl through my body and my eyes felt heavy from the tears fighting the urge to fall. We walked a bit further through the forest until we found the statue near the trail. I turned my flashlight off and sat down against it, my back cool against the stone. Cole turned his flashlight off and placed his hand on my shoulder as he leaned down in front of me. In the dim light of the moon, his facial features were barely visible. The soft, blue moonlight lit up the side of his face, slightly revealing his eyes, nose, and chin. I reached my hand forward, feeling the rough hairs piercing through his skin. His hand moved from my shoulder to my neck and crawled up onto my chin, our faces mirrored in the moonlight. Cole's face must have been inches away because I could feel his warm breath against my lips. I whispered his name, acknowledging the two of us at that moment. He began to say mine before a sound in the distance brought us both back to the harsh reality of what was happening around us.

"That must be Seraphina," Cole whispered, rustling through the dirt for his flashlight.

"Cole," I said, placing my hand on his arm, "Please be careful."

He didn't turn the flashlight on after discovering its location, but instead stood up using the moonlight to find the dirt path, "I'll be back soon and we can go back to whatever reality it is we want to live in."

And with that statement, he walked off into the night, whispering Seraphina's name as if he were summoning her instead.

Creatures of the Night

  I swallowed my fear, listening to the sounds of the dark forest engulfing every living thing in its wake. So much time had passed, I was losing patience and the urge to sleep began to take control. I shook myself awake, slapping my cheek every so often in order to remain vigilant.

  Where the hell is he? I thought, remembering how dangerous this entire situation truly was. I tried to listen for any human sound, but I couldn't hear much over the insects buzzing and the howling of a coyote in the distance. I threw my hood over my head and tried to wrap my arms around myself to keep warm. I didn't plan on the cold creeping in so quickly. I thought it was going to be warm enough to sit outside for however long it took Cole and her to fix this.

  As I tucked my feet in close to my stomach, I heard a rustling sound in the trees above. The moonlight was brighter now, illuminating more of the space around me as it grew later and later. An owl began to sing its night song, welcoming the dark and enjoying its peace. I watched the owl as it hung on the branches of a tree for a few minutes before taking flight, maybe to find dinner or just to travel the skies. Watching the ground from high above must look so beautiful. A freedom I wish I felt.

Freedom. I whispered the word to myself. *Freedom.* I was done sitting and waiting to get my life back. I had been sitting and waiting for Cole for the last hour or longer. I lost track of time while listening to the sounds around me. The more I thought about it, it didn't seem fair that I had to be the one sitting outside waiting when Dougal wanted me anyways. I should have been the one to summon him to death. He's the one who wants me. He wants *me*.

While lost in my thoughts, I heard a strange noise and shot up to my feet. Eyes wild, I tried to look around and find the source of the sound. I bent down, running my hands through the dirt in hopes of finding my flashlight. After I retrieved it, I stood silently listening for that same sound again. It was a scraping sound, but it almost sounded as if something were walking nearby. I tried to quiet my nervous breathing, but all I could hear was my heart thundering in my chest. A few moments went by when I heard it again, scraping. It sounded as if someone were dragging their feet through the dry dirt. I knelt down by the statue, flashlight ready in hand to be used as a weapon.

Without noticing, my hand was covering my own mouth as tears flooded my eyes. It was Dougal. It was the demon I had named and it was standing only a few feet from me. His form appeared taller in the moonlight and his arms were hanging down immensely, his fingers touching the dirt path. His slender body wasn't even illuminated by the light of the moon, but instead by the darkness of his being. He was darker than the darkness surrounding us and his mouth seemed to gape. Unsure of what to do, I stayed in my position, my knees burning from having knelt down so oddly against the statue. He stopped for a moment, peering around through the forest before he began to drag himself toward the castle once more. His long fingers were scraping against the dirt, creating a small dust storm to fly up into the air. He looked as if he were floating like a balloon at a child's birthday party.

Dougal was a creature of the night and in that moment, hiding in the dark, watching him drag his eerie body toward the castle, I guess I was too.

I know I should have stayed where I was, but curiosity got the best of me once more. Standing now, I watched him glide through the doors and disappear into the entrance of the castle. I took a deep breath, frightened yet determined to end all of this here and now. Cole was now in danger and I knew that if things got bad, I would need to be the distraction to save him.

Instead of using the dirt path following in Dougal's footsteps, I snuck amongst the dark trees weaving in and out before making my way to the castle wall. It looked monstrous in this light and the bricks felt cool against my cheek. I stood quietly and listened for movement expecting to hear noises from within, but heard nothing.

Witches

 I stood in silence, still listening for some type of movement from either outside or within the castle walls. The silence was eerie and honestly kind of creeping me out. I would have expected to hear something after seeing Dougal enter the enormous structure. I began to tiptoe quietly, my hand sweeping across the damp bricks. The cold gave off a sense of calm and relief, but this situation was neither. I searched for the window I had entered before and found it, a briar bush growing just underneath. My flashlight had been off this entire time and somehow, it seemed as though I knew exactly where to go. This place was growing all too familiar and although I loved the castle, I didn't find much enjoyment in this whole process.

 I began to climb, placing my feet in the same familiar cracks from my last encounter. Taking a deep, but silent breath, I crawled up the side of the castle and pushed my body through the window.

 The room I fell into felt damp and the smell of mold was heavy in the air. I listened for voices as I knelt down in front of the window in case I needed to make a quick escape. Again, I heard nothing. With the annoying silence and lack of Cole's being, I stood up and brushed the dust off my knees. I squinted hoping it would help me see, but all I saw was the dark red carpet leading me to the old staircase.

The floor began to creak as I made my way through the doorway. When I finally reached the bottom of the staircase, I looked up to find the same large hole in the ceiling, dripping with dark water. The carpet was wet and my feet sloshed with each step I took. I ascended the stairs carefully, stopping every few steps to listen for any sound of movement that was not my own.

When I reached Dougal's floor, the same familiar smell met my nose and I was immediately nauseated. This time the smell had a tinge of iron which could have been blood. I put my hand up to my face covering my nose and mouth before continuing down the moonless hallway. When I reached the doorway, it was closed and the small holes from before still remained throughout the door itself. I stopped, listening in for the voice of Cole. I figured this is where he would be by now since it had been so long since I've heard anything from him. I stepped forward and put my ear against the door, but once again, heard nothing. Agitated, I placed my hand on the door and pushed it open. It scraped against the old wooden floor as it slid, accidentally announcing my presence.

I walked into the room and everything looked as it did weeks ago when I first stumbled upon it. There was a candlestick in the window, dusty books lying in the corner of the room, an old pillow on the floor, and the drawings on the wall remained the same. I took a deep breath, smelling the familiar moldy smell and walked over to the books on the floor. I knelt down, running my hand over the cover of the one I had taken.

Lost in nostalgia, a voice whispered from behind, "You seem to enjoy snooping in this room."

But, I didn't turn around. I kept my eyes focused on the books in front of me, my fingers curling at the ends.

"Did you not hear me?" A quiet voice questioned, "I am right behind you."

Then, there was a giggle.

I began to quickly whisper to myself. There were a few things I had learned throughout my studies that could alter the path I was about to bring myself down when I finally faced him again. I felt a finger poke into my back and turned around to see Seraphina smiling at me.

"What was that you were just saying?" She asked, eyes wide.

"It was nothing." I said, shrugging off the fact that she touched me.

She began to speak again, but I hushed her to quiet down. She looked confused, "That didn't sound like nothing… that sounded familiar."

"Why were you sneaking up on me like that? I could have hurt you." I said, tucking my hair behind my ears.

"I thought it would be funny," She laughed, looking around the room a bit more closely.

"Where's Cole?" I asked, trying to change the conversation as fast as I could.

Ignoring my question, she spoke with a sly, knowing glance, "You were just reciting a spell!"

"You don't know what you heard," I said, standing up, trying to move past her, "Now can we go find Cole?"

She shrugged again, "He told me to come up to this room to prepare for the demon's arrival."

Confused, I questioned her, "Well, what is he doing?"

She smiled and said, "Wow, you care a lot more about Cole than I thought you did. I would love to see his face when he finds out there are two witches who could put a spell on him!"

"What are you talking about?" I asked, squinting my eyes as I scanned the eerie room behind her.

She smiled and pointed directly at me. "You're a witch," she said. She flipped her hair to the side, "Cole mentioned you and how you're like totally pissed off about all this demon stuff, but I don't see how that's true when you're a witch yourself."

Then, moving her hand to point at herself, she added, "And I'm also a witch."

I shook my head, "I don't know what you're talking about, but we need to go find Cole."

"Alright, witch, let's go find him then," she whispered. I could see the corners of her lips curl up, her face squishing together as she smirked at me in the dark.

...

"Pick up the pace," I whispered, turning around to check on Seraphina as she played with a flame in her hand.

"Do you see what I'm doing, *witch*?" She asked, giggling to herself as she ran her fingers along the flame to make it change colors.

I had a feeling she was scared of me by the way she kept calling me 'witch' instead of my real name. It seemed as though something inside of her changed when she saw me in that room, whispering to myself quietly in the corner. It felt powerful. It made me feel powerful. If my presence was growing to make Seraphina feel inferior, maybe I could use that against Dougal and rid this place of him for good. Maybe Cole would be impressed by what I had done, and realize this Seraphina girl was as rotten as an apple.

"Ouch!" Serphina yelled behind me as she tripped over something on the dark hallway floor.

I hushed her and reached for her arm, but she pulled away before I could grab her. I stopped and looked at her, her eyes glowing in the dark, "I'm fine, and don't touch me," she said.

I shook my head and rolled my eyes, turning back around to continue down the long, eerie hallway. She and I could never be friends. She was abrasive and rude, and seemed to think she was better at living than I was. I'm not exactly sure what Cole saw in her or why he started spending time with her in the first place. He said it himself that she wasn't any good to be around, so why would he keep wasting more and more of his time? I rubbed my hand over my face and took another step before coming to an abrupt stop.
Seraphina walked into me as if she wasn't paying any attention, "Ow, what the hell are you doing?"

I shushed her again before asking, "Wait, do you hear that?"

There was complete silence for a moment before I heard a quiet breath come from the room to my right. I turned my entire being toward the door and gently nudged it with my fingertips. It was stuck against the floor and I used my hand to push it harder. It began to move as it creaked and scraped against the old, wooden floor boards. Seraphina tried to get by me, but I put my arm out to stop her, my gaze still completely fixed on the now open room in front of me.

"What is that?" She said, sucking in a breath as if fearing for her life.

"Dougal," I said, raising my hand as if I were about to take him on alone.

Before I could say another word, Cole burst out from a connecting door to the left of us. He rushed toward Dougal, the light in his hand going out as he moved quickly across the room. There was so much sound all at once that I thought my ears were going to bleed. The smashing of glass, someone screaming, and the hissing of the wind all clouded my ears and I couldn't feel my feet enough to move. I stood frozen, trying to see what was happening in the pitch-black room. Seraphina must have made her way around me because before I could do anything, a light burst from within the room and her face was immediately illuminated brighter than the sun. Cole was standing by an old, wooden chair closest to me, while Seraphina stood by a shattered window across the room from Dougal himself. I, still standing in the doorway, took in the moment, trying to think of what the best plan of action was because the one we had before was clearly not going as planned.

"ENOUGH!" Seraphina yelled, louder than I had ever heard her speak.

"Enough? I find that funny coming from your mouth," Dougal hissed.

Seraphina shot me a puzzling look before returning her gaze to Dougal, "That's enough I said."

Dougal let out a monstrous laugh, bringing his long, skinny arms into the air above his head, "Who are you to tell me anything?"

Seraphina adjusted her feet carefully, "I created you, so I can boss you around as I please."

"Stupid girl, you're nothing but a mere human made of flesh and bone!" Dougal blurted angrily.

Cole and I made eye contact as he moved closer to me as I stood still in the doorway, barely crossing the threshold. He looked scared and uncertain, exactly how I felt watching Seraphina and the demon she had summoned speak to one another in a chaotic fashion.

"You don't need to hurt anyone, Sathrion. Let it go." She demanded, reaching her arm out toward him.

"Do not speak my name!" He screamed, his eyes now glowing a deep red as he gazed upon her.

I felt Cole's fingers grab hold of my hand, squeezing it as if indicating he was going to protect me against whatever was about to happen. Seraphina had used a different name to confront the demon I had called Dougal for so long. Being the one who created him, I'm not surprised she had given him a name, but why would she have not shared his true name with us before coming here? I felt a small bead of sweat running down my forehead and I lifted my free hand to wipe it before it reached my eye, but my movement attracted Dougal, who was now staring at me. I tried to speak out, but it was as if my mouth was sewn shut and my eyes suddenly filled with tears.

The demon began to speak softly, a grin forming on its face, "What's the problem, witch? Are you scared?"

Cole stepped in front of me, breaking my eye contact with the demon, "You will not speak to her again."

The demon laughed again, this time exposing his sharp, yellow teeth, "Is this so, boy?"

Cole did not answer, but I felt his grip loosen on my hand and I tried to hold on tighter. His whole body began to shake and I heard myself scream as he fell to the floor. He continued shaking and I knelt down next to him, putting pressure on his body to stop the shaking.

"Stop!" I screamed, tears running down my face.

"Stop? Stop what?" Dougal hissed, moving closer to Cole and I both.

Seraphina stood by the window, looking as if she didn't know what to do.

"I hope the guilt eats you alive!" I screeched, pointing my finger toward her while the other held onto Cole, still convulsing on the floor.

Seraphina let out a squeak, pressing her hand to her mouth. Tears streamed down her face and the flame glowing in her other hand hissed as they dissipated amongst it.

"It's a shame," the demon said as it began to speak once more, "that your friend will die here and you'll be stuck with the pain of not being able to save him."

I took a deep breath, my hand still feeling Cole's body shake. I've been angry before, furious even, but I've never felt the way I was feeling at this very moment. There was a sudden sharp pain in my lung and my ears began to ring. I broke my gaze from Cole and looked toward the demon, now standing above me, drool dripping from the sides of his gaping mouth. Seraphina seemed to take a step back in shock or fear, as if what she was seeing was something from a movie scene or a story book.

I brought my hand to the floor and stood up, making the demon move his face back away from mine, "You are weak."

Standing about 8 feet tall, he titled his head, his red eyes still glowing, "I am anything but weak, my dear."

"I doubt that," I said, feeling a smile forming at the corners of my mouth.

"Why does she look…" Seraphina began to speak, her voice shaking, but the demon silenced her with a wave of his long, spindling arm, sending her sailing back against the broken window. I heard her let out a screech of pain, but I couldn't bring myself to break the stare the demon and I had with one another.

Cole stopped moving against my leg, and although I was trying to keep my composure, I felt cracks in the hard shell I was forming.

"Ah, death is a dark and evil being, don't you agree?" The demon said, looking down at Cole and then back up at me.

"Your death will be." I said, shakily, smiling as tears rolled down my cheeks.

The demon smiled once more, eyes wide, maggots falling from his mouth, "I cannot die if I am already dead."

"Then I will bring you back," I said, shivering at the thought of it.

Behind the demon, Seraphina was bringing herself to her feet, grabbing hold of her side. She couldn't stand up straight, but she forced herself up, leaning against an old bookshelf near the window. I broke my gaze with the demon, and stared at Seraphina in confusion. She smiled at me and then her mouth began to move as if she were speaking, but I couldn't hear what she was saying. She reached her hands forward, bloodied and shaking. The demon turned to face her, an angry frown forming as he turned his head down toward her.

"Do not make me angry, girl," He spoke aloud as the room began to shake.

His body moved so fast throughout the room I almost couldn't see it as he reached out toward her. There was a bright flash and I closed my eyes completely, covering my face with my hands. I heard a loud thud and when I opened my eyes, Seraphina was bloody, lying lifelessly on the floor, but in front

of her was a man.

Never Cross a Witch

The man lying on the floor began to move. He stretched back and forth, extending his arms and legs from the fetal position he was in. His hair was dark, black even, and he wore something that resembled a cloak. It was so long that it covered his body like a blanket. I stood frozen, my gaze switching between both him and Seraphina's lifeless body. I was unsure of how I was able to see in the dark room, but a blue light was shining and snowflakes began to fall from the ceiling above. My heart was beating rapidly and I brought my hands to my chest, unable to breathe. Unsure of what to do, I knelt down to Cole who had lost all color in his skin. His hair began to gray and I tried to wipe the tears that were pouring down my cheeks. I placed my hands on his arm and laid my head down gently on top of his body. I cried for what felt like years until the shock of someone touching my shoulder snapped me back into the true horror of reality.

When I looked up, I saw the dark-haired man standing over me. I leapt up onto my feet and fell back a few steps before gaining my balance.

"Stay away from me!" I screamed, "I do not wish to be here anymore!"

The dark-haired man looked around the room at both Seraphina's lifeless body and then down at Cole's, "I do not wish to be here anymore either now that my queen is dead."

I wiped my tear-soaked eyes and sucked in a breath, my voice quivering, "Queen?"

The dark-haired man pointed his long, spindling finger toward Seraphina's lifeless body and within an instant, it began to dissipate. The snowfall stopped and ashes were left in the space her body had been.

He turned to face me and spoke quietly, "You are alone now. Are you scared, witch?"

I stepped over Cole's body, careful not to touch him with my foot. I sighed, making eye contact once again with the dark-haired man who now stood in the space the demon once resided.

"Dougal," I said, "I don't care who you are, what your reason was for being here, or where you came from, but you will not stay here any longer."

"Is that so?" He said, smiling once again revealing his sharp yellow teeth, now dripping with blood.

I closed my eyes, reaching my hand forward, trying to remember what I had learned. When I first snuck into the castle, I spent a lot more time here than I had ever let on. I spent hours reading the stories found in the dark room where I had met Dougal. The pages of the books were soaked in blood and the images on the walls were all encompassing. I lit a new candle each time I entered the room and didn't leave until it melted itself down into a pool of cold, hard, wax. I drew myself there, a young woman, full of uncertainty and despair. I stole the ritual guide book to read it and learn more about other worldly beings. I was terrified, yes, but I was also studying to learn more about who I was and what to do with myself. I practiced witchcraft in my bedroom and placed spells amongst people I saw in the coffee shop I frequented. I felt powerful for the first time in my life, and yet, I felt weak and unappreciated. I fell in love with darkness, and an interest to decipher it, to befriend the demon's in my life. Cole, the boy I had snuck out to see when I was young, was a darkness in my life, yet his aura was lavender-colored and soft. I whispered to myself, feeling a heat against the palm of my hand. I opened my eyes to the horrid sight of Dougal's skin falling away from the bone. He let out a scream as tears fell from his eyes and within an instant, his body melted into a pool of cold, hard, ash.

    I stood there, in the dark, silent space, staring at the ceiling. The room was lit with one million stars and they sparkled with heavenly light. I knelt down next to Cole, rolling him over to face me. I whispered into the space between us and my tears met his skin with a small splash. He sucked in a heavy breath and coughed before reaching his arm out to touch me.

I reached down, smiling back at him, brushing the ash from his cheek, "Cole?"

His face was flushed, hot and pink, but he let out a laugh as he said my name, "Elia."

A witch. What a powerful and beautiful being, where the darkness of the unknown dances with the light of nature and ancient wisdom.

Made in the USA
Columbia, SC
06 January 2025

fe9859eb-7377-4604-ae13-b27aa4e95fa6R03